Wondrous YOU

EMPOWERING POEMS FOR MAGICAL KIDS

Kayla Floyd

Ordering Information:
Quantity sales. Special discounts are available on quantity purchases by corporations, associations, and others. For details, contact Kayla@KaylaFloyd.com.

Illustrated by Ellen Newcomb

Wondrous You/ Kayla Floyd. —1st ed.

ISBN 978-1-7354870-0-7

For Chloe,

Thank you for inspiring me every day.
You being you is pure joy.

Introduction

These poems were born out of the lessons I have shared with my daughter over the years. They are the same principles I have guided adults through in my work as an intuitive and a meditation teacher. Whatever our age, it's always the right time to remind ourselves that we are loved, we are worthy and who we are matters.

Use these poems as conversation starters to help your child begin to think critically about the world around them. I believe it's our job as parents to create a foundation of love and safety while gently guiding our children to look within their own hearts for the answers to life's questions. The earlier they are able to distinguish between their own inner knowings and the outer messages thrust upon them, the better.

I encourage you to look within your own heart as well as you share these words with the little ones in your life. Invite your own inner child to sit with you and offer them a chance to be seen and heard. It's never too late to heal ourselves, and it's never too early to empower our children.

May you find your beautiful, powerful self mirrored back to you within these pages. And may the children you share this with feel deeply seen and deeply heard.

What a joy it is watching you grow
In a body as magical as each flake of snow.
I treasure gazing in your wide, knowing eyes
And celebrating each milestone passing with time.

And while I love this body that guards your heart,
I want you to know that it's not really who you are.
You are so much more than skin and bone.
You're a soul, an essence, a song that feels like home.

Your body is a helper, there to carry you through life.
Its job is to work with you and protect you from strife.
You must nurture it and love it and know its role,
But never confuse it for the you that is your soul.

The world will tell you that outside is what counts,
That the physical body is how you amount.
But know that this is all completely untrue,
And look instead to the energy inside you.

Root for your body; be patient and kind.
Tend to its needs and nurture your mind.
But remember, my love, you aren't your skin.
You are the life force that lives within.

Your voice is more than the sound that comes out.
More than a whisper, more than a shout.
It's the you that sees life in your very own way,
The you that has important things to say.

Your voice helps to make you unique.
It's the special way only you think.
Feelings that matter and opinions that count,
Your voice carries a story you need not discount.

Some voices make art and others make books.
Some voices build structures and others fashion looks.
Some voices rally troops and others go within.
Your voice will guide you, so listen, lean in.

Your voice is a tool to use with care,
But never be afraid to lay your heart bare.
Use your words to tell your truth.
Share your knowings; share all of you.

Follow your feel-good, do what makes you smile.
Be your own person, have your own style.
You're here to be the most YOU that you can,
And your voice has always been part of that plan.

CONTRAST IS YOUR FRIEND

Have you ever noticed that life can feel tough?
Moments of pain, days that feel rough.
Sometimes sadness overtakes your whole self,
And you wonder if or when you'll ever feel well.

These times are not meant to last, my dear.
Things will get better; the fog will clear.
Just as night moves to day and dark yields to light,
Your sorrow will lift; it will all be alright.

These waves of trouble are not all bad.
They're not here to keep you forever sad.
Darkness is a friend in its own way.
It helps us appreciate the light of day.

Opposites teach us what we value most.
Pain constricts us just before love brings flow.
Contrast is a tool that helps us get clear
On what we love and all we hold dear.

So next time you feel the darkness close in,
Invite it to sit with you; give it a grin.
Ask it to guide you, to lead you to truth.
It's there, my love, to help you know you.

Pain is a part of life here on earth.
Bumps and bruises, emotions that hurt.
But pain doesn't have to steal our power.
It doesn't have to be our darkest hour.

Inside each of us, (yes even you),
There's a healing force that knows what to do.
Right in your chest, deep in your heart,
Feel the vibration that rumbles to a start.

With only your thoughts, the energy will sail
From there in your heart to whatever ails.
It doesn't have to stay inside of only you.
You can send this power to whoever is blue.

Sometimes we all need medicine and doctors.
But know that your energy is always a factor.
Find your heart and dive into its well.
Swim in the sweetness; let the energy swell.

Even if your skin stills needs a bandage.
Even if your body sustains some damage.
Know that healing energy flows through your veins,
And its mantra is the sound of your own sweet name.

The body you're in is a gift to you.
It's a helper, a doer, a great friend too.
You can use it for play, for pleasure, for fun.
You can use it for hugging, for laughing, to run.

But remember your body is yours first of all.
When it comes to boundaries, you make the call.
No one should touch it without your consent,
Or offer their opinion or words of discontent.

It's not too skinny, and it's not too fat.
It's not too this, and it's not too that.
Your body is perfect in all its forms.
Its job is to change, not to conform.

It's normal to look different from others.
We are a people of many wonderful colors.
Bodies are as different as each grain of sand,
And yours is glorious right where you stand.

Remember your body isn't who you are.
It's a house for your soul, kind of like a car.
You can decorate it up or dress it down.
You can move it if you want or lie around.

It's not your job to look a certain way.
It's not your duty to make others feel okay.
Live in your skin knowing it's unique
And flaunting your own beautiful mystique.

The words you say are more than you think.
There's power behind them, an invisible ink.
Each word that you utter leaves its own mark,
A lasting trace of either lightness or dark.

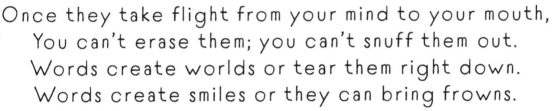

Once they take flight from your mind to your mouth,
You can't erase them; you can't snuff them out.
Words create worlds or tear them right down.
Words create smiles or they can bring frowns.

Choose what you say with the utmost care.
Are you doing harm you'll have to repair?
Is it loving, is it kind, would it build someone up?
Is it needed, is it true, does it make the cut?

Choose to be the person who uses their voice
To make a bold, brave and powerful choice.
Choose to be the one who rises above
And uses their words to speak only love.

YOU ARE ENERGY

You are a spark of pure love and light,
An energetic boom that lit up the night.
Deep in the dark your magic grew,
And out came a miracle - wondrous you.

The energy inside is who you are.
An effortless stream, a bright-shining star.
Your power isn't something you have to earn,
But managing its flow is what you must learn.

Spend time in quiet sensing your vibration.
Open your heart; begin a conversation.
Deep in your gut, you'll feel the hum.
You'll hear the beat of your very own drum.

Find this rhythm as often as you can.
Tap into the energy you have at hand.
Spread outside of the physical you,
And ask to see what's real and true.

Into the dark, you'll take a ride
And find the truth about what's inside.
You'll be taken back to that first little spark,
Right to the center of who you really are.

Remember this trick for all of your days,
When the world seems dark and it's all a haze.
Close your eyes, and feel the buzz.
It's the you who always is and always was.

Everything you see begins as a thought,
One simple intention someone brought
From right in their head, down through their heart,
Off their lips, a creation they start.

Thoughts create things, things we can see,
So choose your thoughts carefully.
Imagine a world, and then live it up.
What you focus on, you become.

Along the way remember to be grateful.
Gratitude is a tool, a device for the faithful.
It helps your body stay in the right vibe.
It helps your dreams find you in perfect time.

Sometimes your thoughts will manifest quickly.
Other times it may not happen as swiftly.
Stay true to your dreams and soft in your heart;
Allow the Unknown to do the mystical part.

Remember your power in the thoughts you keep.
Your beliefs are shaping the world you see.
Choose thoughts of a world where you'd love to live
And give thanks for the one you're already in.

YOUR ENERGY IS A GUIDE

How you feel is a teacher and a guide,
But first you must learn to look inside,
To ask yourself what your heart is saying
And see what your body might be conveying.

Energy and emotions are clues you can use
To see what it is you want to do.
They can tell you if a person is friend or foe;
They can tell you if a choice is yes or no.

Listen to your body and all of its cues.
If your heart yells NO, that's valuable news.
Never do something that feels unsafe;
Never move forward when your body says stay.

Remember your boundaries and trust your gut.
Your energy helps you to know what's what.
Use your words when things feel odd;
It's always okay to take a pause.

Your body is a tool, and your feelings are a friend.
How you feel matters, and plans can always bend.
Be sure to ask for help when your body says no,
And never be afraid to let your feelings show.

There's a secret to getting where you want in life,
A formula for managing all the strife.
It's scattered there at your feet,
The tiny knowings of what you need.

You don't have to have the perfect plan.
You don't have to know the entire span.
Getting yourself from point A to Z
Takes one simple inquiry.

Ask yourself and then allow,
What would feel good to me right now?
It could be a bath, a smoothie or a walk.
It could be a laugh, a movie or a talk.

Long journeys happen one step at a time,
And feeling our feelings is the through line.
No matter what your life becomes,
Always follow your feel-good breadcrumbs.

Don't waste time with worry and doubt
Or stress about how things turn out.
Remember that life is simply a string
Of beautiful moments that make our hearts sing.

Hard work will find you without a doubt.
At some point you'll have to figure out
How to do a task that's extra tough,
And working it out might feel rough.

But just because a job takes time
Doesn't mean we have to lose our mind.
It's all in how we meet the day
And what we let our energy say.

Choose to see a lighter path,
And find a mindset that always asks,
How can I let this be more fun?
Can I invite ease to get it done?

Sometimes the steps might not shift,
And our energy is what must lift.
Bringing joy to what you do
Gives ease a way to flow through.

Let it be easy, let it be fun,
Let it be enough to get it done.
Choose lightness of heart and softness of mind
In every task that you're assigned.

There's a funny thing that happens with time.
Your body grows, and so does your mind.
The world looks different, and you will too.
Change is a constant no matter what you do.

Babies crawl, and then they walk.
Toddlers babble, and then they talk.
Kids learn to color, read and write.
Teenagers drive and ditch the bike.

Sometimes it's easy to want to rush through
And meet tomorrow's version of you.
But growing up is best taken slow.
Enjoy being you, and go with the flow.

There's a thousand tomorrows and yesterdays too,
But there's only one now, only one you.
The person you are as you're reading this
Is the version of you one day you'll miss.

So enjoy being you right here and now,
And learn wholeheartedly to trust and allow.
Have fun being a kid through and through,
And memorize this feeling of wondrous you.